THE INFLATABLES
in BAD AIR DAY

To Gemma, who always pumps us up —BG & JH

To Vanessa, Jaime, and
Vivienne Poet Rodriguez —CD

Chapter One

A Wave of Excitement

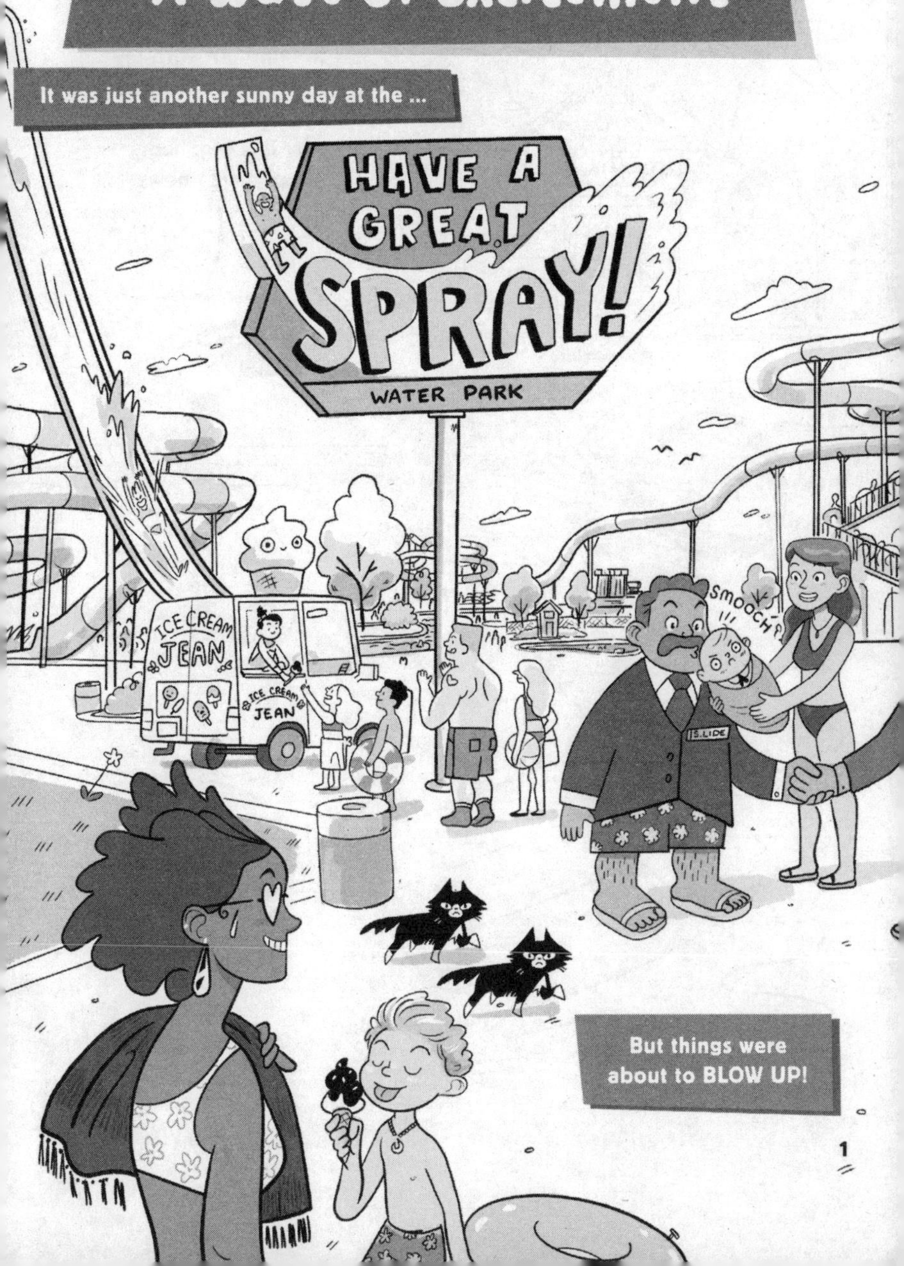

What a lovely day to hang out with my inflata-pals without being interrupted by any big, huge, top-secret news.

3

5

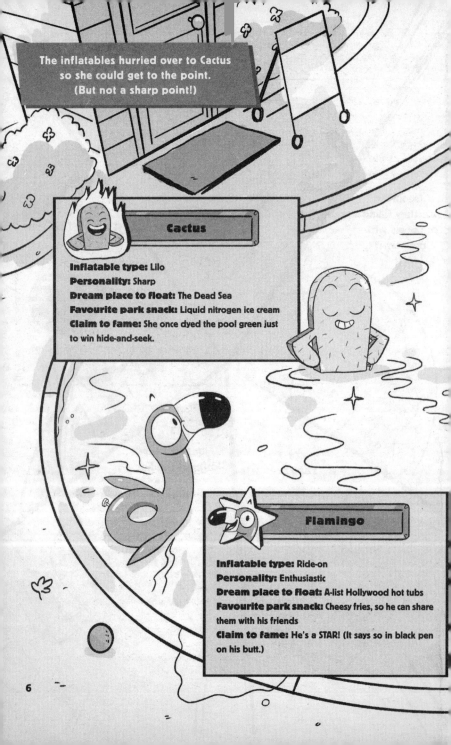

The inflatables hurried over to Cactus
so she could get to the point.
(But not a sharp point!)

Cactus

Inflatable type: Lilo
Personality: Sharp
Dream place to float: The Dead Sea
Favourite park snack: Liquid nitrogen ice cream
Claim to fame: She once dyed the pool green just to win hide-and-seek.

Flamingo

Inflatable type: Ride-on
Personality: Enthusiastic
Dream place to float: A-list Hollywood hot tubs
Favourite park snack: Cheesy fries, so he can share them with his friends
Claim to fame: He's a STAR! (It says so in black pen on his butt.)

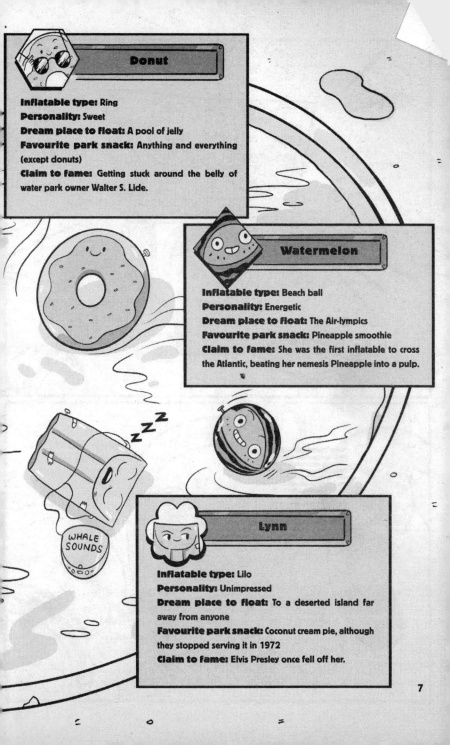

Donut

Inflatable type: Ring
Personality: Sweet
Dream place to float: A pool of jelly
Favourite park snack: Anything and everything (except donuts)
Claim to fame: Getting stuck around the belly of water park owner Walter S. Lide.

Watermelon

Inflatable type: Beach ball
Personality: Energetic
Dream place to float: The Air-lympics
Favourite park snack: Pineapple smoothie
Claim to fame: She was the first inflatable to cross the Atlantic, beating her nemesis Pineapple into a pulp.

WHALE SOUNDS

Lynn

Inflatable type: Lilo
Personality: Unimpressed
Dream place to float: To a deserted island far away from anyone
Favourite park snack: Coconut cream pie, although they stopped serving it in 1972
Claim to fame: Elvis Presley once fell off her.

Oh my goggles! It's Walter's big plan for the park!

Yup! And guess what? There's a ginormous new wave pool opening ... TODAY!

9

10

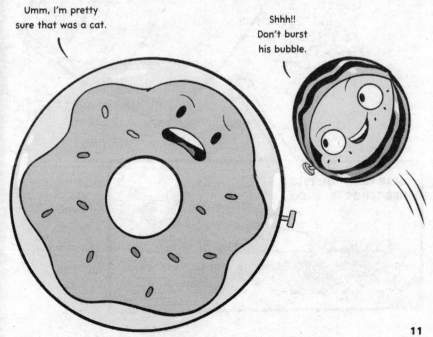

13

Donut loved inventing tasty combinations.

Fries cream: What's better than ice cream? French fry–flavoured ice cream!

Woofles: Waffles + hot dogs + candyfloss, the paw-fect combo!

PopDogs: Popcorn + gummy worms + bun = the best thing since sliced bread (stuffed with popcorn).

Cooking with DONUT!

THE YUM CHANNEL

It's even better than waves AND snacks! A new pool opening means crowds and celebrities ... and camera crews!

If I can get them to notice me, I can finally fulfil my destiny!!

Um ... you have a destiny?

POKE POKE

Yep, take a look.

IT'S ...
BUTT TIME!

Chapter Three
The Butt of Destiny

Four big letters were inked across Flamingo's brightly-coloured behind.

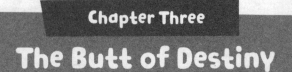

HAVE A GREAT SPRAY! WATER PARK

LOS & FOUND

BRB

S.T.A.R.

See? It's written all over me! I'm supposed to be a STAR!!!!

16

17

But just as Flamingo was imagining his name in lights...

What ...

PLOP!

... the ...

TEE HEE HEE

HE HE

HA HA HA HA

... snow?!

HA HA HA
HA HA HA
HA
HA
HA

HA HA HA
HA HEE

HA HAH
HA HA HA

There's snow EVERYWHERE. And sprinkles. In the middle of summer. It's a magical winter wonderland miracle!

Chapter Four
Vacation Deflation

Chill out, Flamingo. That's just your reflection!

And anyway, what's so scary about a sw—

ARGH! Don't even say it!!!!

But, Flamingo, I don't get it. Those big white birds are pointless!

25

It all started with one AMAZING, UNFORGETTABLE holiday.

Cue the best wibbly-wobbly dream sequence ever.

FAVOURITE FLIP-FLOPS

HEAVY-DUTY SUN CREAM

DRY TOWEL

AUTOMATIC INFLATOR

BANGING TUNES

RHINESTONE SUNGLASSES

RUBBER REPAIR KIT

EXCITING BOOK

NAME: STEVE TARQUIN AUSTIN RODRIGUEZ

28

29

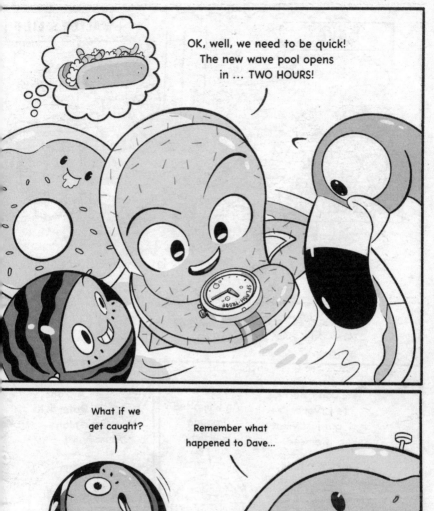

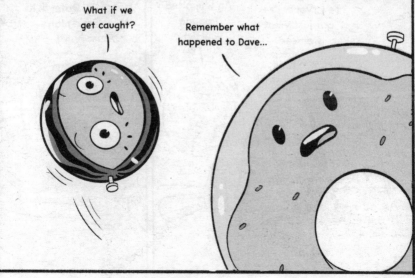

Don't worry, everyone. I've got just what we need.

An unlimited PopDog voucher?

No, Donut. A plan. A watertight plan.

34

39

THE LAWS OF PAWS AND CLAWS

CLAWS
(LOOKS LIKE PAWS)

HAVE A GREAT SPRAY!
WATER PARK

WHISKERS LOOK SPIKY

ICE CREAM JEAN

PAWS OR CLAWS

CLAWS OR PAWS

SUPER-SHARP POPPY THINGS. BEWARE.

LOOKS LIKE AN AIR HOLE, BUT DO NOT ATTEMPT TO BLOW UP.

44

45

46

The Big Let-down

The inflatables weren't shy about letting it ALL out.

FLUUURP!

PAAARRPP

PFFFT

AHHHHHHH

And once again I thank my lucky stars we're right by the bathroom.

47

52

54

And with that, the inflatables were on the move.

Chapter Seven

Freeze or I'll Scoop

Don't worry, guys. We'll never have to sneak around like this again. Once I'm a STAR, we'll only be filled with mountain air and will be carried around on cushions!

Oh my feathers! I think we're there!

SCREEECHH!

And ... we're back!

Oh, I LOVE how she did my wings.

Perfect for showing off my new dance.

It's definitely good, right?

SPLASHY FALLS
JUNGLE WATER SLIDE

LINE

S.T.A.R

Umm ... yeah ... it's ... umm ... great!

60

MY DESTINY IS SO NEAR, I CAN SMELL IT!

Are you sure that's destiny you're smelling?

There was no time to run!

CLAWS

PAWS

And there was barely enough time to hide!

63

66

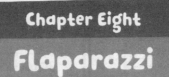

Chapter Eight
Flaparazzi

71

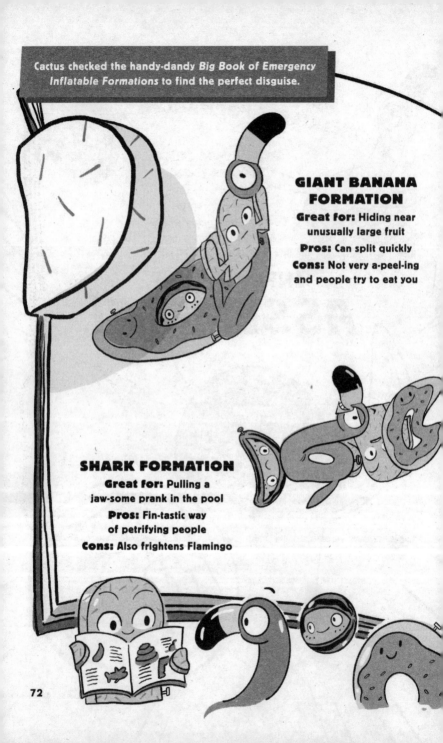

Cactus checked the handy-dandy *Big Book of Emergency Inflatable Formations* to find the perfect disguise.

GIANT BANANA FORMATION
Great for: Hiding near unusually large fruit
Pros: Can split quickly
Cons: Not very a-peel-ing and people try to eat you

SHARK FORMATION
Great for: Pulling a jaw-some prank in the pool
Pros: Fin-tastic way of petrifying people
Cons: Also frightens Flamingo

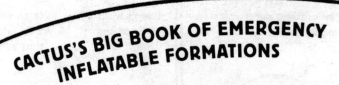

CACTUS'S BIG BOOK OF EMERGENCY INFLATABLE FORMATIONS

BIRTHDAY CAKE FORMATION

Great for: Sneaking into pool parties

Pros: Muffin compares to it

Cons: Last time, Donut bit into a cream-covered Flamingo

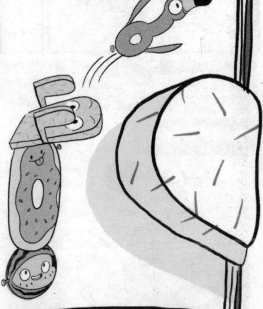

DIVING BOARD FORMATION

Great for: Reaching new heights

Pros: Never a (belly) flop

Cons: Slippery when wet

Formations were perfect for hiding in plain sight. And bringing the gang closer together.

Possibly too close.

75

77

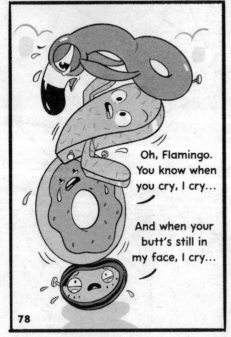

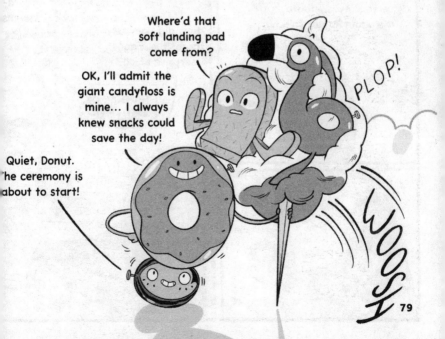

79

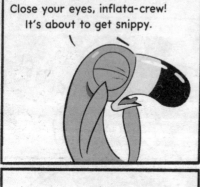

81

Chapter Nine
Swandemonium

Swandemonium was a hit! The crowd went wild!

HELP!!!

So wild, they didn't notice a bunch of fleeing inflatables.

And a flamingo who was about to cry. Again.

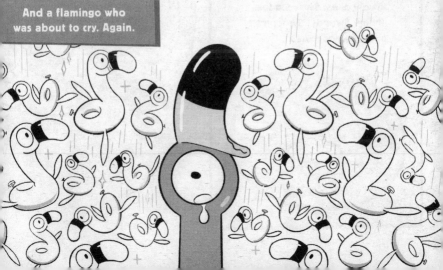

85

Chapter Ten
A Cunning Plan-cake

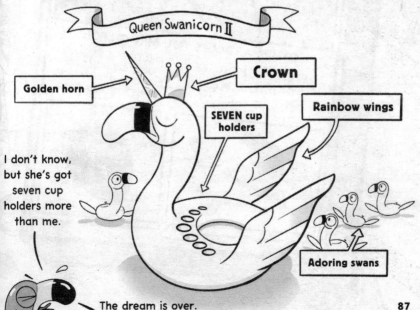

Queen Swanicorn II

Golden horn

Crown

SEVEN cup holders

Rainbow wings

Adoring swans

87

89

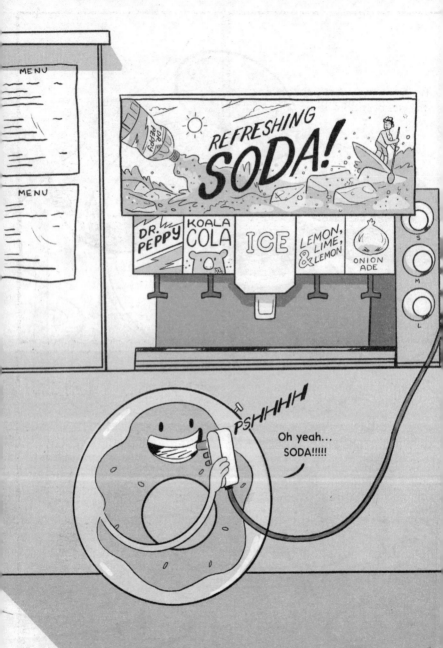

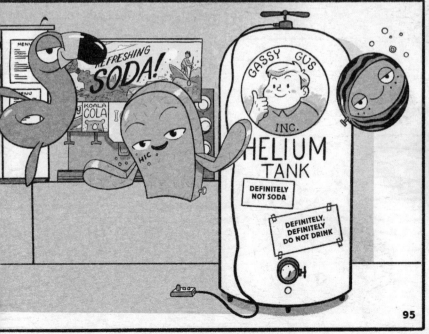

I can't believe you guys. You gave up waves and slides and PopDogs for me. And you didn't complain once.

I don't even need to be a star when I've got friends like you. YOU'RE my destiny.

I promise to be braver next time. For you.

ON TOP OF THE WORLD!

TERRIFIED ANTS

SWANDEMONIUM WAVE POOL

97

99

So they told Lynn the whole story.

Well, almost the whole story.

LOST & FOUND

They skipped the part about Walter's swan swimming trunks.

100

101

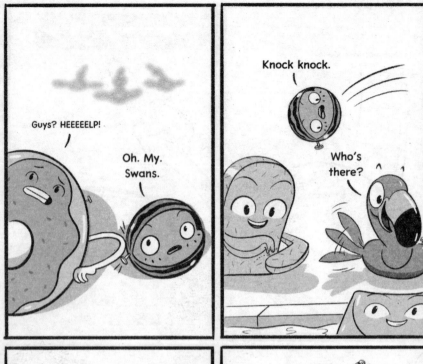

102

104

109

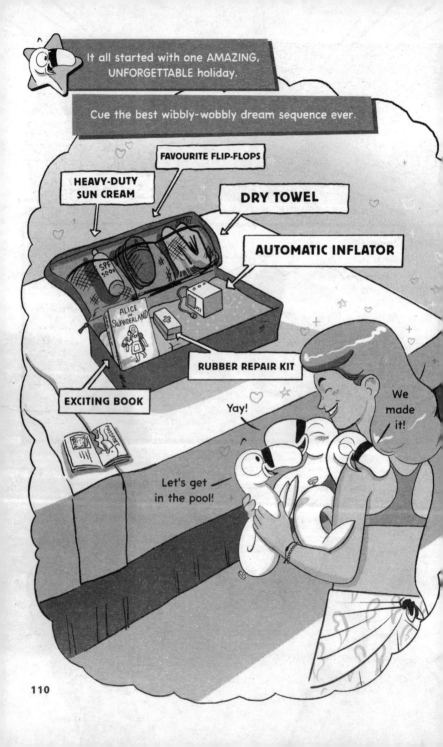

111

Guys! All this time you
only wanted photos?!
Why didn't you just ask?

Who's ready to beak-dance?

IT'S FLAMINGO IN THE HOUSE
IT'S FLAMINGO IN THE POOL

IT'S FLAMINGO IN THE PLACE
AND I'M FEELING PRETTY COOL

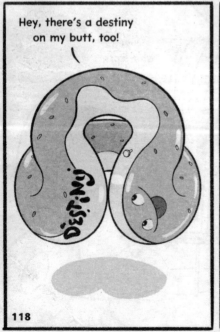

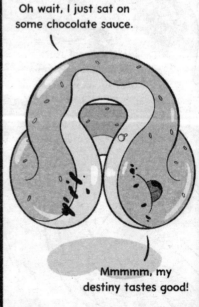

To the greatest ever writer, my mum −JH

For Daddles, the original and best storyteller −BG

To my fiancé, my adventure partner, and the
love of my life, Eva. I love you more
than Donut loves snacks. −CD

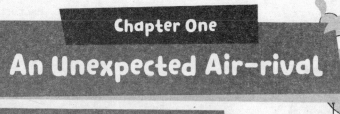

Chapter One
An Unexpected Air-rival

It was another sunny day at the Have a Great Spray Water Park. And Cactus was taking it easy.

Just kidding. Cactus was busy making air-mazing inventions for her inflata-buddies!

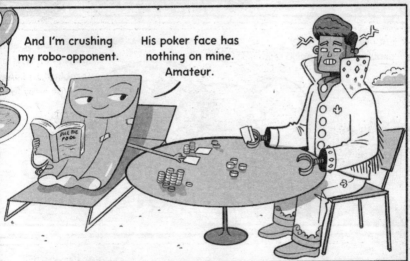

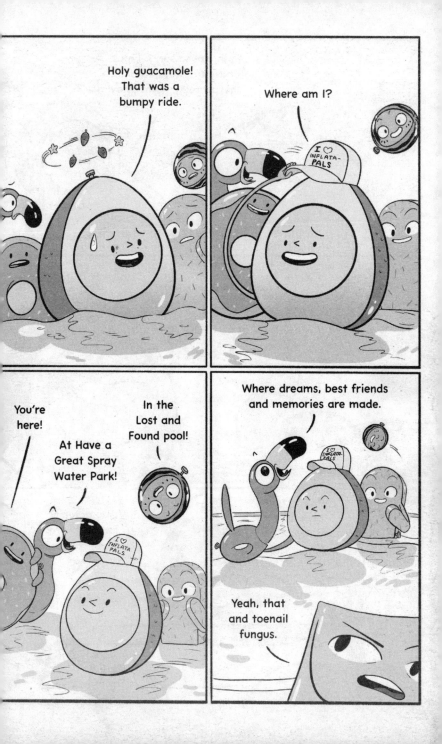

135

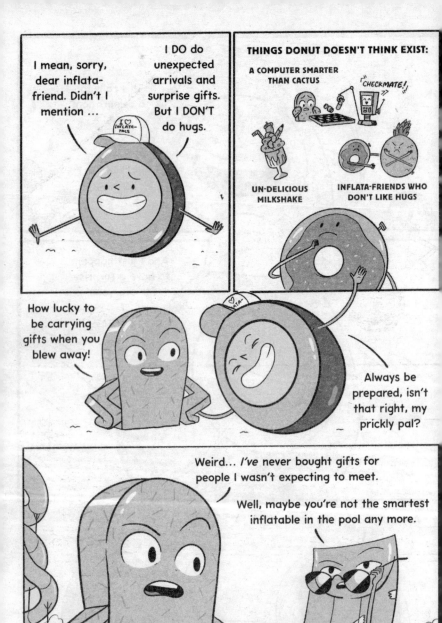

136

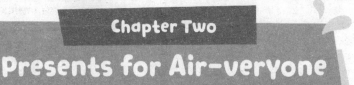

Chapter Two
Presents for Air-veryone

Sweet! I normally have to buy surprise gifts for myself. Wait! I think I forgot my July-versary!

Your what?

DONUT'S MONTH-IVERSARY GIFTS (TO HIMSELF)

JANU-VERSARY

FEBRU-VERSARY

MARCH-VERSARY

APRIL-VERSARY

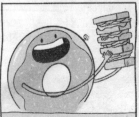

EXTRA-APRIL-VERSARY

MAY-VERSARY

137

138

139

140

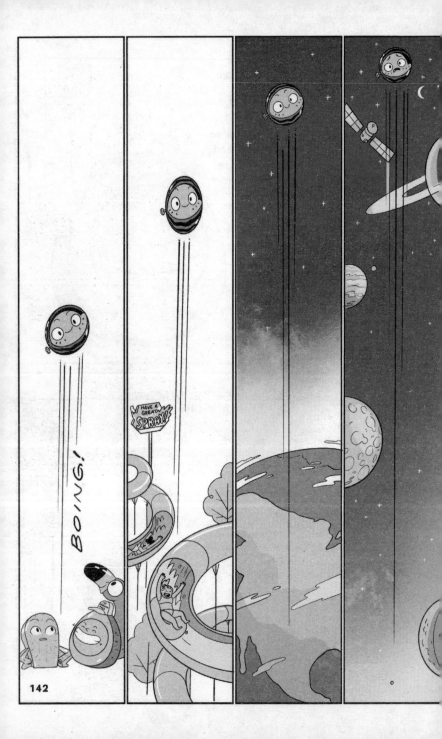

143

Now you can bend into any shape you like!

FLAMINGO
MODELLING KIT

No. 27 | SUPER CUTE PUPPY!

STEP 1: PUT YOUR HEAD BEHIND YOUR TAIL.

STEP 2: TUCK YOUR LEFT WING BEHIND YOUR NECK.

STEP 3: SAY "I LOVE AVOCADOS" THREE TIMES.

I LOVE AVOCADOS, I LOVE...

STEP 4: POINT YOUR BEAK TO THE LEFT.

STEP 5: TA-DA! YOU'RE A PUPPY.

SPECIAL **BENDY** MODELLING SPRAY INCLUDED

144

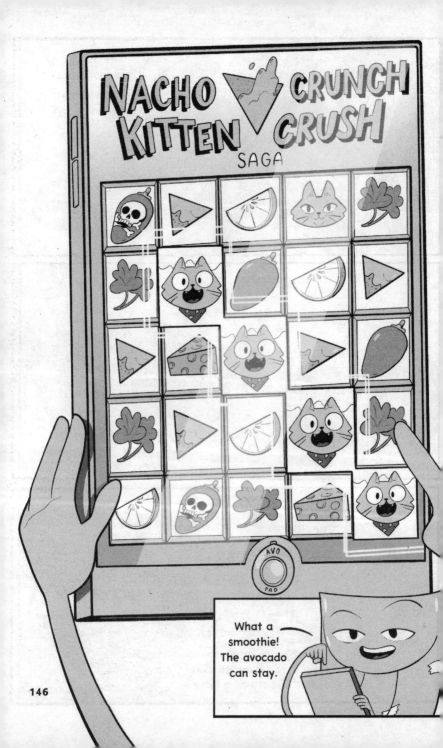

147

148

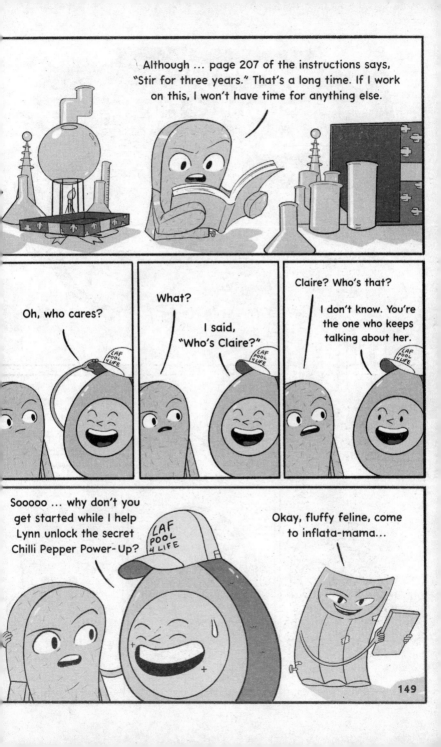

149

Chapter Three

An Air-Raising Experiment

Cactus was in her element.

THE WORLD'S MOST COMPLICATED SCIENCE EXPERIMENT

155

156

159

Chapter Four
An Air of Mystery

Cactus was feeling deflated. But she had a point to prove.

Has anyone seen Avocado?

BE BACK SOON! Love from your friendly Avocado xoxo

He said he had to do something normal and un-suspicious, and went thataway.

WOBBLE WOBBLE

Weird coincidence! That's just where I was heading...

WOBBLE GOGGLES Can see around corners, above buildings, and down water slides

STAFF ONLY
WALTER S. LIDE'S
SWIMMING TRUNKS
COLLECTION

WOBBLE GOGGLE
EXTENDED MOD

What IS he avoca-doing?

Avocado might be a fruit full of nutrients, but he's up to something. Well, here goes nothing...

Hello-oooo-hhhhh? Is there an unexpected yet totally welcome stranger in here?

Mysterious. I thought I heard someone snooping around.

And if there's one thing Avocad doesn't like, it's snoopers. Or huggers. Or smoothie blenders.

GUL

And don't get me started on smelly balls of fur with air holes under their tails. What's the word for them? Oh, yes ... cats.

Here, vile smelly-welly. I mean, cute kitty-catty. Eat this and stay away from me. I've got evil plans to be getting on with.

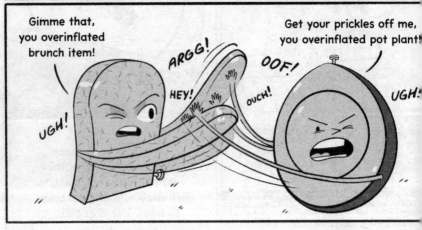

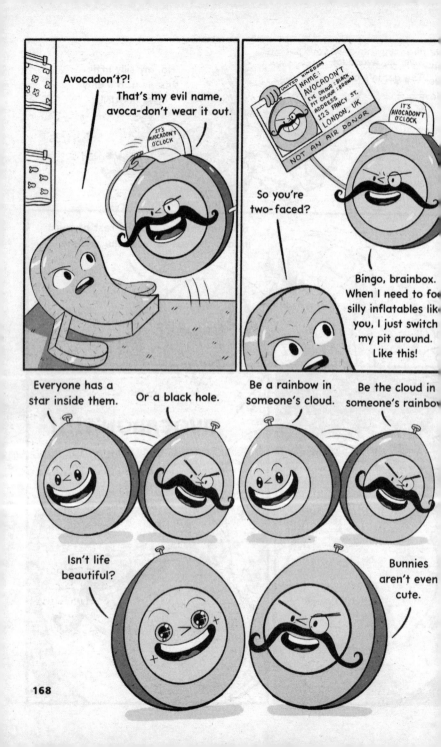

168

169

Chapter Five
Oh, No You Avoca-don't!

Inflata-pals!! Hold on to your air holes! You'll never believe what I just discovered!

Avocado ISN'T an innocent inflatable! He's an EVIL MASTERMIND! With a surprisingly long moustache!!!!

AND HE PLANS TO TAKE OVER THE PARK!

Um ... anyone?

Well, I for one am furious.

You made me miss grabbing the golden nacho! I've been stalking that sucker for hours.

But there is no excuse for a surprisingly long moustache.

173

174

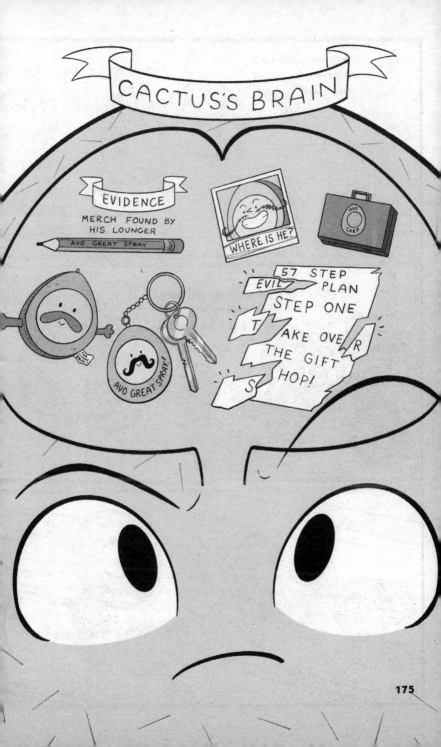

176

-179

THE LAWS OF GNAWS AND JAWS

181

PILLOW FIGHT

WATER FIGHT

STARING CONTEST

THUMB WAR

183

PUPSICLES + MAGNIFYING GLASS + SUN =

SLIPPERIEST GOOP TO STOP AVOCADON'T

LAP LAP

SCHLURP!

185

186

Chapter Seven

Eggs-It Through the Gift Shop

You put your air hole in! You put your air hole out!

You put your air hole in! And you shake it all about.

You do the Floaty Pokey, and you turn yourself around.

GUYS!! THIS NOT WHAT IT ALL ABOUT

We don't have time for silly dances. Avocadon't has gone to the gift shop to take over the world!

Dude, he's probably gone to the gift shop to pee.

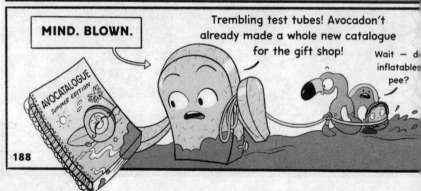

MIND. BLOWN.

Trembling test tubes! Avocadon't already made a whole new catalogue for the gift shop!

Wait — d inflatables pee?

AVOCATALOGUE
SUMMER EDITION

188

AVOCATALOGUE
SUMMER EDITION

AVOCOPTER

AVOCARD DECK

AVOCADOORS

AVOCARDIGAN

AVOCAR

AVOCADOG

AVOCADODO

192

196

Chapter Eight
Total A-pop-alypse

197

So how do we stop Avocadon't?

We need to find out what his secret weapon is and block it!

TRAIL OF GREEN GOO

So, who's ready to follow that fruit?!

I'm iced and ready for action!

Count me in!

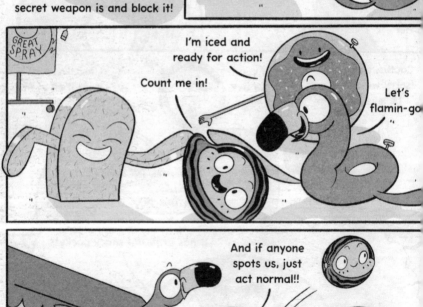

Let's flamin-go

And if anyone spots us, just act normal!!

GIFT SHOP

You're too late! While you air-heads were following my fake footsteps, I sent Walter an invite to my party tonight. Once he tastes my Hypnotic Guac, he'll say yes to whatever I want and hand over the key! Soon all this will be mine, all mine ... with a dash of lime!
HAVE A GREAT SPRAY!
AVO GREAT SPRAY
S.LIDE
Well, maybe I don't need the changing rooms. Too many soggy plasters.
Think again! There's still time before the party starts for us to cook up an antidote to your unholy guacamole.
AVO GREAT SPRAY
PLOP

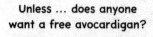

Unless ... does anyone want a free avocardigan?

Silly me! I forgot to hide the Big Free Avocardigan button.

BIG FREE AVOCARDIGAN BUTTON

It's right by you, Donut. One press and you'll get free avocardigans for life.

And did I mention hot dogs, too?

NOOOOOOOO!

AHHHHHHH!

SLAM!

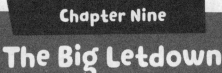

Chapter Nine
The Big Letdown

The Avo Great Launch Party has started! Come and celebrate at the Big Splash Pool!

Oops.

Oh dear. That *wasn't* the free avocardigan button. It was the Start the Launch Party button. Silly me.

GOTCHA!

See you later, inflata-duds. Oh, and one last thing...

GOTCHA!

Prepare to be popped!

WAVE

HYPNOTIC GUACAMOLE

And the party looks ... fun. This is air-rendous.

Don't be sad, Cactus.

You did everything you could!

Avocadon't is just the evilest fruit and/or vegetable EVER!

He doesn't even like hugs.

Or not popping his only friends in the world.

211

C'mon, Cactus. There's nothing a Donut hug can't fix. Well, maybe it can't make an Avocado go soft, but...

You're right. Avocadon't may have an impressively evil brain—

And a great cap collection!

But I have one thing he doesn't ... you guys! And while there's air left in us, we still have a chance to save Have a Great Spray!
There's only one thing left to do.
Three ...
two ...
one...
INFLATABLES, ASSEMBLE!
Refill the dip!

It's Nacho Park Any More

Welcome to MY party. I hope you have a mesmerizing time!

AVO GREAT SPRAY
LAUNCH PARTY

IT'S AVOCADO JEAN.
LIVING THE AVOCADO DREAM.
WITH MY DE-PITTING MACHINE.
AVO GREAT SPRAY!

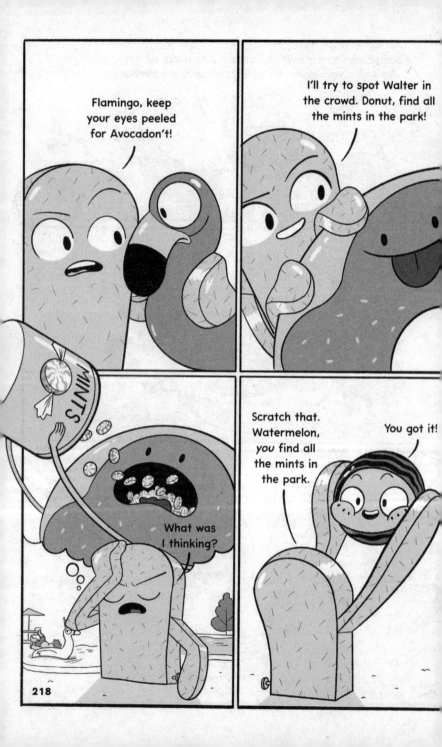

CAN YOU FIND...

☐ Walter's spare flip-flop

☐ Gift Shop Shelly's skateboard

☐ Queen Swanicorn's newly added eighth cup holder

☐ Paws and Claws

☐ Gnaws and Jaws

☐ Ice Cream Jean

☐ Avocado Toast

☐ 'Cado Coaster

222

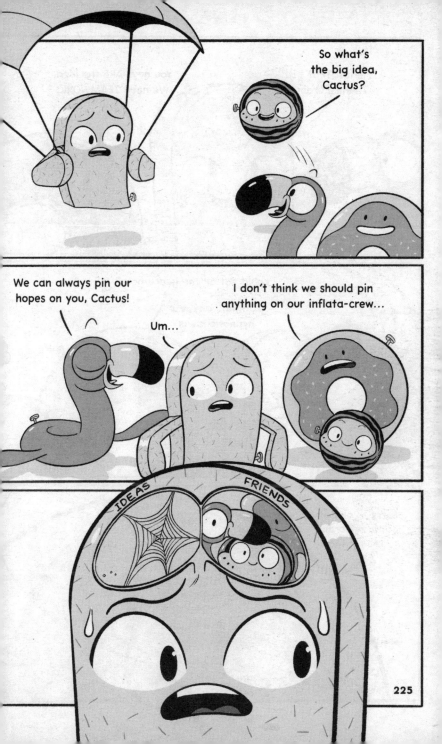

225

Friends! That's it!
Thanks, brain.

WINK

You guys ARE the idea.
We need TEAMWORK!

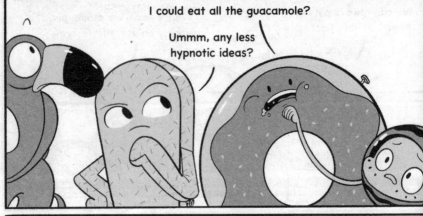

I could eat all the guacamole?

Ummm, any less
hypnotic ideas?

Sorry — all I've
got in my brain
is ... jelly.

SWOOSH

What about making the world's biggest whirlpool? I could whip one up with my super-speedy skills?

I would help but I was trying Balloon Shape Number 53 – Avocado Masher and now I'm stuck like a statue.

Chapter Eleven

Jello! Is It Key You're Looking For?

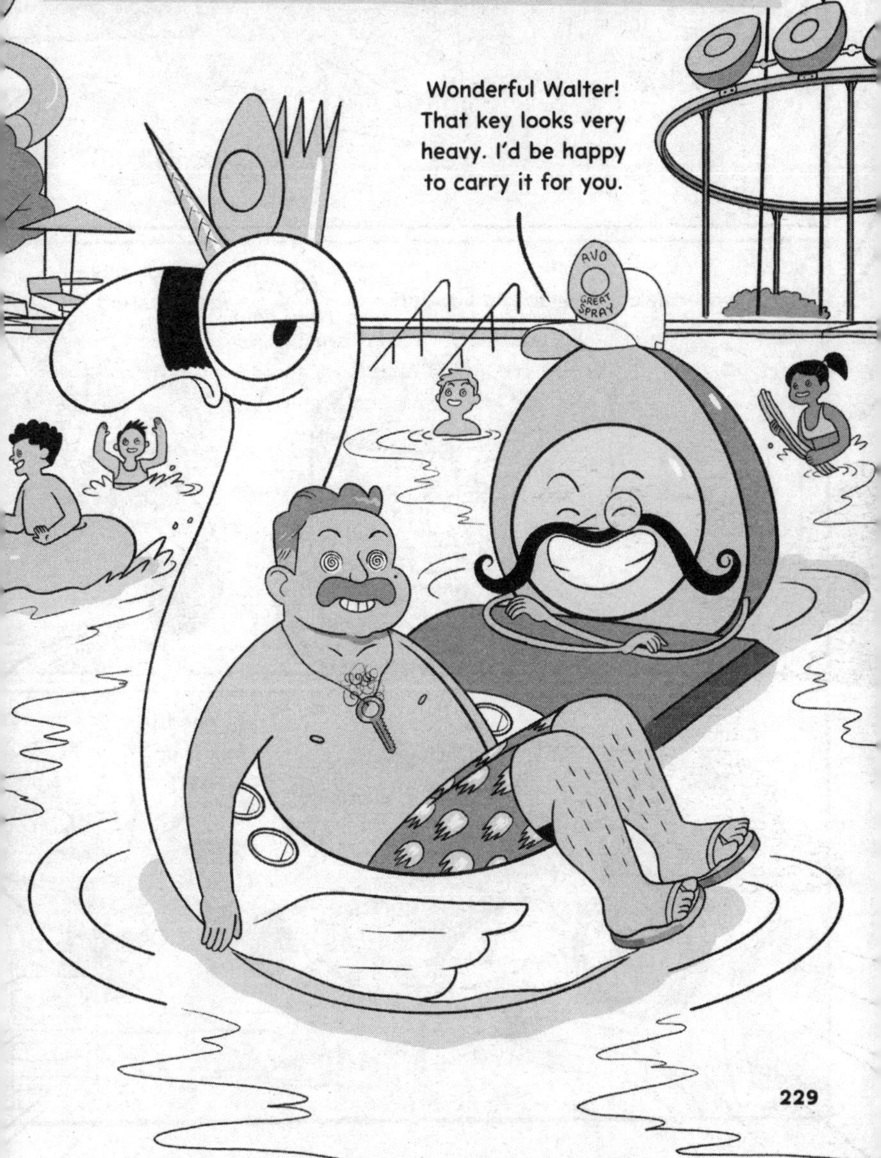

230

My game's glitched. And you're the only inflata-genius that can fix it.

We're kind of in the middle of saving the water park here!

Yeah. Avocado is really evil ... and he's hypnotized Walter ... and he's about to hand over the key to Have a Great Spray ... and we turned the pool into jelly ... but now we gotta get the key first ... and it's too sticky to walk on!

STATS

So what I'm hearing is that you need me to build you a path to Walter?

Yes, but we've only got seven seconds before the jelly melts!

234

236

238

Chapter Twelve
Happily Avo After

And the inflata-gang lived happily avo after.

Wait, no. That's just the guacamole talking.

I can't believe that jelly took you a whole week to slurp up, Donut.

I can't believe I still wasn't full.

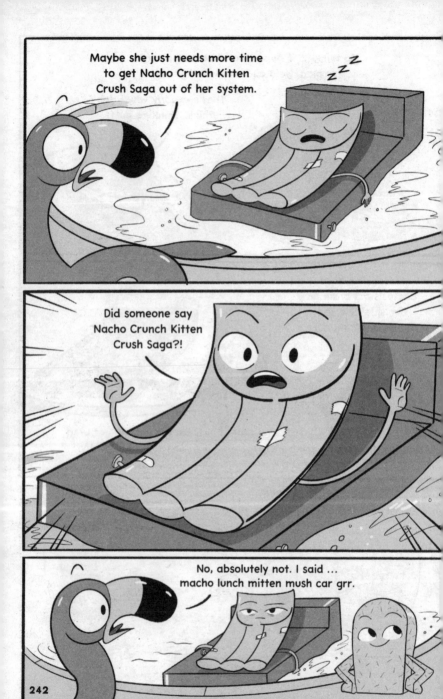

245

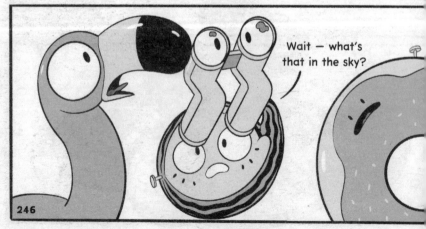

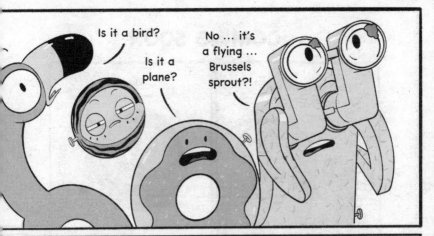

COMING SOON

It's that there's another inflata-mazing
adventure ... starring us!

THE INFLATABLES
in DO-NUT PANIC!

Holey sprinkles! Donut's going on a treasure hunt. The prize? The most delicious cookie ever tasted. But to find it, he needs to sneak his inflata-pals out of the water park, survive shark-infested seas, and take on a petrifying Pickle. Will the holey hero make it back unpopped, or will the cookie crumble once and for all?